Murder by Christmas

Murder by Christmas

MOON'S LANDING COZY MYSTERY SERIES
BOOK SIX

SHELLEY WEISS

 Created with Vellum

Chapter One

ONCE AGAIN, it's Christmastime in Moon's Landing. Every year, without fail, our sleepy little town came alive with the magic of the season. I'd always believed that if there were one place in the world that could completely transform into Santa's Village, it would be this town. Nestled in a cocoon surrounded by mountains and the sea, we might as well be cut off from the rest of the world. But we take Christmas seriously —no corner was left undecorated.

Each year, my neighbors would try to outdo the other by dressing up their lawns and homes with the latest blow molds and twinkle lights. This town had everything, but one particular detail was always missing—I've never seen it snow here.

Walking down my street was just a glimpse of what the rest of the town had to offer. As I crossed, I admired a house wrapped in glowing white lights threaded through tree branches, the trunk covered in red foil with a giant gold bow. Presents, carefully wrapped, sat beneath the tree, waiting.

Next door, a grand Victorian house held wooden reindeer in the windows, while the roof was covered in painted turf to mimic snow. Faux-glass ornaments in shades of blue and gold sparkled against the white.

And then there's my other neighbor, Mason Whiskey Moon; his home remained untouched. He must not have received the H.O.A. letter informing us that our homes needed to be decorated to show our spirit. But, knowing Mason, I don't think he was afraid of our president, Lois Jones. Not many knew she embezzled H.O.A. funds. I couldn't prove it, at least not yet.

My coonhound, Butterscotch, and I barely got one final walk in this evening before I needed to go to work. As the only photographer for Moon's News, I was sent to cover anything and everything, and tonight would be no different. The assignment is to photograph the grand opening of our local Museum of History, and I've been looking forward to it all day.

I've always loved museums, losing myself in daydreams about the artifacts and fossils they housed. Who used these items? What were their lives like? But tonight, I had no time for such thoughts. I had a job to do.

Leaving Butterscotch at home with a new chew toy, I hailed a cab to the museum. The streets were draped in starburst motifs and candy-cane tinsel, every building adorned with wreaths and bows. As we rode, I glanced up at the dark sky, closing my eyes for a moment to wish for something that had eluded Moon's Landing for as long as I could remember —snow.

"What's it like?" The driver asked, pulling me from my thoughts.

"What's that?" Unsure about what he asked me about, having been lost in my daydreams.

"The party at the museum," he clarified. "I'd never been to one of those. I heard Philip Jones is giving a speech."

Philip Jones, running against Deputy Brent Lomack for

sheriff, was known for playing dirty, with Lois helping him run his campaign. Deputy Lomack, on the other hand, was trying to keep things fair, though I'd told him that now wasn't the time for niceties. Another Jones in power would be disastrous for Moon's Landing.

"If you like, you can come in with me," I offered. "And grab a bite to eat."

His eyes lit up with excitement. "You think that will be okay? I don't want to get you in trouble."

I waved the concern away. "It'll be fine."

We pulled up to the museum's drop-off zone, and after paying him through my phone app, I waved goodbye. He promised to park and meet me inside.

I had my favorite camera with me tonight, a Rolleiflex 2.8B. As I checked the settings, I nearly slipped on the slick steps leading to the museum doors. Luckily, Mason Moon caught me just in time.

"Careful," he said, steadying me. "The ground's wet."

I gave him a grateful smile. "Thanks. That could've been bad."

"I was just on my way out," he said. "Came by to speak with Lomack."

"Deputy Lomack?" I asked, surprised.

He nodded. "Gave him a check for his campaign."

"I hope he wins," I said, my concern obvious. "But why aren't you staying for the party?"

He gave a wry smile. "I avoid parties if I can. They involve people."

I laughed. "Generally, yes. But it's Christmas."

Mason pulled out a gold pocket watch, an heirloom from his great-grandfather, Whiskey Moon. I'd seen it many times before, though as far as I knew, it hadn't worked in years.

"Did you get that fixed?" I asked.

He shook his head and tucked it back in his pocket.

"Nope. Doris Gilbert's inside. She's been trying to corner me for an interview. I was hoping to avoid her."

I glanced at the sky again. "I just wish it would snow," I mused. "It would make everything perfect."

"Snow?" Mason chuckled. "It's not all it's cracked up to be."

Just then, Blanche called from the museum doors. "Birdie, there you are! I texted you ages ago!" She waved me over. "Hurry! I want you to get a shot of Deputy Lomack next to the Christmas tree."

I turned to Mason. "Blanche has been playing campaign manager," I explained. "She's determined to see him win."

The rest of the evening moved quickly as I got to work. I took a photo of Lindsay Zimmer, who was catering the event, and was surprised to see Stevie Mitche and Josh Lomack working as her event staff.

"Hey, Birdie," Deputy Ben Griffins waved me over. "Mind snapping a picture of my fiancée and me by the tree?"

I hadn't recognized him at first without his uniform. He looked sharp in a dark blue suit, his hair slicked back like a 1920s gangster. His fiancée, Ashley Oliva, was equally striking in an orange cocktail dress.

"Of course." I happily posed them, making sure the over-sized bows on the gifts framed the shot just right. The big band hired for the night began playing a jazzy tune, and I swayed a little as I moved away, smiling.

Across the room, Mason stood watching. He caught my eye and gave me a small smile before disappearing into the crowd. It seemed he had decided to stay after all.

Chapter Two

As I stepped into a back hallway to reload my camera, I heard voices arguing nearby. Though I tried not to eavesdrop, I couldn't help it when I realized who it was—Deputy Ben Griffins and his fiancée, Ashley. They were in an office just off the hallway, the door ajar.

"Why did you have to mention that to my boss?" Ashley's tone was sharp. "You know she doesn't like you."

"I was just being polite," Ben replied, sounding strained. "I didn't think saying hello would offend her."

"That's not the point," she snapped. "Lois wants everything perfect for her uncle's campaign. Just being here with Lomack has her fuming."

I fumbled the empty film canister, which clattered loudly across the floor. "Oh!" I murmured, trying to disappear as both of them turned to stare. Ashley flushed, while Ben tugged at his collar, clearing his throat.

"Sorry—I didn't mean to intrude," I stammered, gesturing to my camera.

Ashley let out an exasperated sigh. "No worries. Actually,

Lois wants you to take a photo of her and Mr. Jones with the mayor by the tree."

"Sure thing."

Ashley threw one last look at Ben before hurrying back to the party, her expression tight. I held my camera and tried to shake off the awkwardness of the encounter. Ben lingered a moment, watching her retreat.

"Do you shoot weddings?" he asked suddenly, raising an eyebrow.

"Not usually," I replied with a laugh. "But I can refer you to someone."

He chuckled. "Thanks, but if it were up to me, we'd just elope to Vegas."

I cleared my throat, rushing to explain what I was doing at the door. I still felt awkward about it. "I didn't mean to eavesdrop. I was just looking for a quiet spot to reload my camera."

"No worries, Birdie," he said with a warm smile. "You probably saved me from a longer lecture."

"I didn't realize Lois is Ashley's boss."

"Lois is the museum director," Ben said, surprised. "She's been here over fifteen years."

"Oh, I had no idea."

Ben nodded toward the door. "I better head back. You should check out the silent auction in the Egyptian room—they've got some neat items."

"Thanks, I will." As he left, I bent down to pick up my runaway film canister, which had rolled further down the hall than I'd realized.

I found myself outside a door labeled *L. Jones*. Without thinking, I tried the handle—locked, of course. Maybe Ashley had a key in her office? My curiosity prickled, and I hurried back to Ashley's office, hoping to find something useful.

My search was cut short by my phone buzzing. It was

Blanche, probably wondering where I'd disappeared. I sighed and made my way back to the party.

Blanche zeroed in on me instantly, cocktail in one hand as she grabbed my elbow with the other. "Where have you been?"

"Reloading my camera. Where do you need me?"

"I've rounded up Deputy Lomack and Mason by the Christmas tree," she said, pointing. "I want a photo of them together. It'll be on the front page tomorrow."

"Does Tennessee know about this?" I asked cautiously. "He said he wanted the paper to stay neutral."

"He'll see the logic," she said dismissively, pushing me toward Lomack and Mason. Just then, her face went rigid. Tennessee had entered the party with Josephine Gamble on his arm. "What are they doing here?"

"Are you okay?" I asked, worried. Tennessee and Josephine's relationship was new, and Blanche and Tennessee had been engaged until he broke it off.

Blanche handed me her drink and slipped outside through a side door. I followed, feeling the sharp chill of the evening air hit my face. She stopped by a stone water feature, a mermaid holding a trident.

"You'd think I'd be used to seeing them together by now," she muttered, snatching her drink back and taking a deep gulp. "I'll be fine. I just need a minute."

We stood quietly for a moment. She dabbed at her eyes with a cocktail napkin and took a deep breath. "Let's go back in."

Just then, a delivery driver came rushing toward us, a box in his hands. He spun around, seeming slightly lost. "Excuse me, do you know where I can make this delivery? I've never delivered to a museum before."

"Who's it for?" Blanche asked.

"L. Jones, Museum Director," he replied, reading off the box. "It's a special delivery."

"She's inside," I said. "We're headed back that way, too."

"Oh, thank you kindly," he said, shaking both our hands. "Name's Karl Smith."

"Help yourself to the buffet," I suggested as we walked back in. "The museum went all out."

"That's mighty generous," he grinned. Then he hesitated, glancing inside. "You know, I think I forgot something in my truck. I'll be right back. This Christmas rush has my head spinning."

Blanche and I stepped inside just as Tennessee appeared with Josephine at his side, her arm lovingly draped over his. She eyed us coolly.

"Oh, Birdie, Blanche," Tennessee greeted. "Are we social-izing on the job?"

Josephine smirked, sipping her champagne. "It must feel strange to attend as the *help*, but you two seem to be managing just fine."

Mason approached quietly from behind her. "They're the reason this party is running smoothly," he said.

"Oh!" Josephine gasped, startled. She turned to face him, placing a hand on his chest as she steadied herself. Her eyes softened as she looked up at him. "You have the most unusual eye color. Has anyone ever told you that?"

"Josephine," Tennessee cut in, his jaw clenched. "Let's get back to the party."

"Yes, of course." She let her hand fall slowly, still smiling at Mason as Tennessee led her away.

Chapter Three

A HANDFUL of guests stood outside, gathered around cocktail tables set up for those brave enough to endure the winter chill. Stevie balanced a tray of empty glasses as she maneuvered between them.

The terrace was lined with tall evergreen bushes, acting as a natural privacy fence. I snapped a few photos as I approached her. "I didn't know you were still in Moon's Landing. I thought you headed back to Los Angeles after the musical production *Moonshine Over My Heart* closed." Stevie was the makeup artist.

Stevie smiled, adjusting her red vest, which matched the other staff uniforms with its golden embroidered ornaments along the neckline, black slacks, and polished black shoes. "That was the plan, but Josh told me how nice it is to spend Christmas here. I've actually grown to like this town."

"It does that," I said, nodding in agreement.

Just then, Josh hurried over, leaning in to whisper, though I could still overhear. "Don't look now, but Doris Gilbert is headed this way. She's looking for you."

"Me?" Stevie asked, her eyes widening. "What for?"

Josh shrugged and motioned toward the door as Doris stepped outside. "I'll cover your tables if you want to go hide."

"Hide?" Stevie looked alarmed but didn't wait for further encouragement. She slipped away down a side path leading off the terrace.

Doris's sharp eyes found me. "Was that Stevie Mitche? Where did she go?"

"She just needed to get back to the kitchen," Josh replied, lifting the tray Stevie had left behind. "Now, if you'll excuse me, I need to get back to work."

"Not so fast," Doris stopped him, holding up her coffee cup. "Do something about this drink. It's gone cold."

"Your coffee?" he asked, inspecting the cup. "What's wrong with it?"

"It's cold. I would expect better from Lindsay," she snapped.

Josh took the cup from her, assuring her he'd bring a fresh one.

Doris glanced at me with a huff. "Can you believe it? I just poured that, and it's cold."

At that moment, Mason appeared on the terrace, holding two glasses of a warm, red-hued drink. He offered one to me with a smile. "Deputy Lomack's going to give a speech."

Doris rushed off, calling after someone.

"Oh, I need to get inside for that!" I panicked, pushing the glass back to him. "I thought it would be later."

"There's still time, Birdie." He held the glass out again. "This is just for us."

"What are we toasting to?" I raised the glass, inspecting the contents. It looked thicker than champagne, with a reddish-gold center that reminded me of liquid fire. "Is this from your brewery?"

He nodded. "It is. I'm opening a microbrewery in town,

and this will be served there. You're one of the first to try it. I haven't decided on a name yet."

Curious, I took a sip. The drink had a fruity, slightly tangy taste—a perfect blend of raspberry and pomegranate. Before I knew it, I took another sip. "It's delicious."

An idea sparked, and I handed him back the glass, positioning him holding the glasses. "Stand right there."

"What?" He looked slightly uncomfortable as I lifted my camera but didn't move.

"Hold still," I said, snapping a quick shot. "These photos might be worth something someday."

Mason chuckled, looking down at the glasses. "What do you think of the drink?"

Before I could respond, Lois Jones suddenly appeared from the side path, almost knocking me over. She rushed by without a word.

"Lois?" I called, confused. "Are you alright?"

She barely acknowledged me, disappearing through the door back into the party.

"What was that about?" I asked Mason. But we didn't have time to speculate; a woman's scream rang out from the path Lois had just come down. "That sounded like Doris!" I handed my half-empty glass to Mason and hurried toward the sound.

"Birdie, wait," Mason called, following me.

Doris stumbled out from behind a bush, her face ghostly white as she nearly ran into me. "Birdie! Mason!" she shrieked. "There's been a murder!"

Chapter Four

"A MURDER?" I stared at Doris, stunned. "What happened?"

Mason stepped around us, intending to investigate, but Doris grabbed his arm, pulling him back. "Don't go," she whispered, her face ashen. "We have to wait for the police—the police, Birdie, you need to call them. I can't handle it. I need to sit down."

"Doris, take a deep breath." I softened my voice, keeping her calm. Over her head, I caught Mason's eye; he gave a slight nod and then went to retrace her steps down the path. I led Doris back to the terrace, where a cluster of guests waited, eyes wide with curiosity.

"Birdie," Blanche rushed up, blue eyes darting between us. "We heard a scream. Was that Doris?"

I scanned the crowd, noting Lois's absence, but caught sight of Deputy Lomack pushing his way through. "Birdie, Doris, what's going on?"

"Deputy Lomack, thank goodness," Doris leaned heavily against me. "There's been a murder. Right here." She gestured towards the bushes where Mason had gone. "Mason's back there now."

"Mason?" Lomack's expression sharpened with concern. "Where exactly?"

Just then, Mason emerged from the foliage and waved Lomack over. He looked intent on keeping the guests calm. I guided Doris to a chair, where curious onlookers closed in, firing off questions.

"Birdie," Blanche murmured, stepping close. "What did Doris see?"

"She claims to have found a body," I whispered. "She said someone's been murdered."

"Murdered?" Blanche echoed, following as I moved towards the bushes. "But why would she—"

"Birdie, Blanche," Lomack's firm voice stopped us. He and Mason stepped from the greenery, Lomack's face grim. "Stay where you are. I don't want anyone trampling evidence. This is a crime scene now."

Mason blocked our view, arms crossed. "Let's head back to the party, alright?"

Blanche was not pleased. "We're members of the media, Mason. We have a right to know what's going on."

"You'll do as instructed," Lomack snapped. "Keep everyone away while I secure the scene. Mason—find Griffins and send him over. I'll need help."

"Understood," Mason nodded, leading us back. "Best to follow orders."

Blanche grumbled but went along. "Since when do you take orders from him?"

We returned to the group, where Philip Jones intercepted us, his expression dark. "What's going on here?" he demanded. "Where's Lomack?"

"I told you," Doris was shouting to anyone who'd listen. "There's been a murder!"

Philip's face went pale. "A murder?" Without another word, he darted past us toward the bushes.

"Wait!" I called. "That's not a good idea!" But he was already gone.

As we returned to the terrace, guests peppered Doris with questions, crowding around her chair. Blanche pushed through them, shooing people back. "Give her some space!"

Blanche offered Doris a hand. "Come inside, Doris. You'll feel better sitting down."

"Yes, anywhere but here." Doris looked shaky. "Maybe I should just go home. Can you drive me?"

"Or to the office?" Blanche suggested. "We can talk privately there."

"Privately?" Doris paused, suspicious. "This isn't going to be a story about me, is it? Doris Gilbert is never the story."

Ashley appeared, offering a comforting hand on Doris's shoulder. "You can use my office. There's a sofa if you need to lie down."

"Oh, that would be wonderful," Doris sighed, clutching her head as they guided her inside.

I touched Blanche's arm, stopping her. "Are you sure you want to question Doris? She's got a flair for the dramatic."

Blanche nodded. "I just want her account of what she found. Besides, you can wait here and hear what Lomack has to say when he's finished."

She left, trailing after Doris and Ashley, and I stayed behind. Lomack soon returned—but he wasn't alone. In his hands was a small, disheveled white dog, its fur matted and smeared with dirt. The poor thing looked scruffy, it looked like a Pekingese mix, and it trembled in Lomack's arms.

"Where did he come from?" I reached to pet the dog, but it snapped at my fingers, and I drew back.

"Same reaction he gave Mason." Lomack shook his head.

"Where's Mason?" I asked, looking around.

"He was right here a minute ago." Lomack shrugged. "You must've just missed him."

"What are you planning to do with this little guy?"

"I was hoping you might take him," Lomack replied, holding the dog out slightly.

"Me?" I looked at the growling bundle. "I don't think he likes me very much."

At that moment, Griffins appeared, striding up the path from the parking lot. "Deputy Lomack, we've got a news crew out there wanting a statement from you." He eyed the dog warily as it barked sharply at him.

Lomack sighed, clearly frustrated. "Call Blanche. She's handling the campaign, so she can deal with the press—and maybe the dog too."

Chapter Five

BLANCHE WASN'T THRILLED about dog-sitting, but surprisingly, the little guy only seemed to like her. Unlike everyone else—except for Deputy Lomack—he tolerated Blanche's presence. With no leash on hand, Blanche had to carry him, and though she made a face, she didn't seem to mind it too much.

"What are you going to call him?" I asked.

"What?" She raised her eyebrows in surprise. "Why would I call him anything?"

"You might be holding onto him for a while," Ashley chimed in. "He doesn't seem to have an owner."

Blanche looked concerned. "I don't know about long term—Birdie, I think you should take him until we find his home. You already have Butterscotch—what's one more?"

I shrugged in defeat. "He doesn't like me." Right on cue, the dog growled, warning me I was standing too close. "But he still needs a name."

"A name?" Blanche held him out, studying him closely. Her eyes narrowed. "Hmm...what about Jelly?"

"Jelly?" Ashley chuckled. "Why Jelly?"

"He reminds me of a jelly roll. Round and fluffy."

Ashley tilted her head, amused. "What about Snowball? He's kind of round like one."

"Birdie, what do you think?" Blanche asked.

"Well, if he's yours for now, I'd say call him what you like best."

Blanche nodded, satisfied. "Then Jelly it is."

At that moment, Deputy Griffins hurried over, out of breath. "You need to get over to Deputy Lomack. Philip Jones is wiping the floor with him in front of the press."

"What?" Blanche nearly dropped Jelly in my direction, but his growl stopped her. "I need to see what's happening." With Jelly secure, she followed Griffins to where the press conference was taking place in the museum's parking lot.

I wasn't about to miss this and followed close behind. The coroner was moving the body into the back of a van, the slam of the door echoing across the lot. He looked startled by the noise and quickly muttered an apology to those nearby.

Philip Jones stood front and center among the news crews, basking in their attention. Lois Jones stood off to the side, a thin smile on her lips.

"It's far too early in the investigation to release details, but I can assure you—I will not rest until we uncover the truth."

"Do you suspect murder?" an eager reporter asked, thrusting a microphone at him.

"At this time, it's premature to say," Philip replied smoothly. "But my department is committed to finding out."

"Well, Mr. Jones," Blanche called from the sidelines, Jelly sitting comfortably in her arms, "I think we'd all like to hear from Deputy Lomack. He's the man the people of Moon's Landing trust."

Philip didn't miss a beat. He smiled, unfazed. "Trust me when I say the good people of Moon's Landing deserve accountability. For too long, crime has escalated in what was once a peaceful town."

"That man will not give up the podium," Ashley muttered beside me. "Do something, Blanche."

Deputy Lomack took the cue, pushing his way through the press. "Thank you, Mr. Jones, for your statements. However, I have my own to share with the good people of Moon's Landing."

Philip hesitated, clearly unready to relinquish the spotlight, and Lois quickly tried to intervene. "Why don't we all head inside?" she suggested with a dazzling smile. "It's cold out. Let's warm up with champagne—there's plenty to eat." She ushered the reporters toward the museum doors, her hands directing them like traffic.

"Really, Lois?" Blanche called out, her voice carrying. "We're in the middle of a press conference."

Lois spared Blanche a sharp look. "Dogs aren't allowed in the museum, so you'll have to stay outside. Sorry."

Jelly growled at Lois in reply.

"Can you believe her?" Blanche muttered.

"Yes," I said. "I can."

Blanche turned to me with a determined look. "Birdie, why don't you go inside? I don't trust them not to monopolize the media with their shenanigans."

I'd been waiting for an excuse to sneak into Lois's office. "I'll see what I can find out," I assured her, slipping past the crowd and through the doors.

"Don't let me down," Blanche called after me.

Inside, Ashley was confronting Lois in the hallway. "What's this about?" she demanded. "Railroading Deputy Lomack?"

"I'm not 'railroading' anyone," Lois argued. "It was cold outside."

Ashley folded her arms. "You're not fooling anyone with

that stunt. Deputy Lomack is a good friend, and I won't stand by while you pull this on him."

"Did you forget I'm your boss?" Lois snapped.

Ashley's eyes narrowed. "And don't forget, *I* know all your secrets." She emphasized her words with air quotes, then walked away toward her fiancé, Deputy Griffins, who was standing beside Lomack. They conferred quietly in a corner, their expressions grim as Philip continued holding court with the media.

Lois's gaze found me then, her eyes narrowing as she noticed my camera. She didn't say a word, but her jaw tightened as she turned on her heel and disappeared down the hall toward her office.

What secrets did Ashley know about Lois? And how could I get her to spill them?

Chapter Six

WHO NEEDS an alarm in the mornings when a coonhound wakes you up? "What is it, Butterscotch?" I asked, checking the time on my bedside clock.

Butterscotch jumped off the bed, landing gracefully on her paws before racing out of the bedroom, expecting me to follow. She liked her breakfast routine at six a.m., which included a brisk morning walk to inspect her kingdom. Was that too much to ask?

Adjusting the handkerchief I'd used the night before to wrap my hair in rollers, I grabbed my robe and slipped it on as I headed downstairs to brew coffee. I had thrown out my aunt's automated single-cup server in favor of a twelve-cup coffee maker.

Butterscotch barked impatiently. "Just a second." I clicked on the radio, which sat on the windowsill above the sink. The DJ had a cheerful voice as he relayed the daily news.

"The Sheriff's Department has officially ruled the death of delivery driver Karl Smith to be accidental. The delivery man attempted to make a delivery but slipped outside the museum."

"No murder here," said council member Michael Selfridge, who'd like to remind us to enjoy this Christmas season. Oh, and don't forget: Boston Bob will be in the studio later today!"

I turned off the radio. "Accidental?" I muttered to Butterscotch as I placed her bowl in front of her. "I don't think so." Hearing that Boston Bob would be at the radio station later did pique my curiosity. It wasn't like Boston Bob from the S.O.S. to randomly visit the station. The S.O.S. stands for the Society of Sanitation, formed by janitors as a national organization, but I had never heard of it before moving to Moon's Landing. I suspected there was more to it than met the eye.

"Birdie?" Blanche called, knocking rapidly at my front door. "Are you up yet?"

I opened the door to find Blanche holding two cups of coffee from Sweetie's Latte Café. I grabbed one from her and took a sip. "How did you know I needed this?"

"Because I've known you since we were kids," she replied, pushing past me into the living room. "Why aren't you dressed yet? Have you had a chance to go over the photos you took?"

I nodded, too busy enjoying my coffee to respond. "I got home late but spent most of the night in the darkroom going over them."

"I need some of them now," she said. "I have an exposé going out tomorrow morning."

"An exposé?" Blanche hadn't mentioned one. "Is it on what happened last night? They're calling Karl's death an accident."

"Birdie, you don't buy that for a second, do you?" she asked.

"I don't, but I heard on the radio this morning that the sheriff's office said it was." I led her into the kitchen, opened the fridge, and found an apple pie Lindsay Zimmer, the owner of Sweetie's Latte Café, had brought over yesterday. I placed it on the counter before digging out two forks and plates and serving two slices.

"I did find some interesting photos last night," I said, sitting beside her.

"You did?" Blanche asked, suddenly more interested in the apple pie than what I had to share. I couldn't blame her; it was from Sweetie's Latte.

"There's a photo of you with Lomack. Lois and Ashley are in the background, and Lois is scowling."

"What's strange about that? That's a normal expression for Lois," Blanche said between bites.

I shook my head. "But it's who she's glaring at that has my interest. Let me grab the photos." Butterscotch finished her breakfast and trotted over to Blanche to say hello.

"Good morning, Butter," Blanche said, patting her head.

It didn't take me long to run down to my darkroom in the basement. The photos were done drying, so I took them off the line and brought them straight to Blanche, who had just finished the last bite of her pie.

"Here they are." I laid them on the island countertop. "But don't touch them with your sticky fingers."

Blanche licked her fingers before using the sink to wash them. "What's so special about those photos?" she asked, glancing at them.

"Look here." I laid three photos side by side to show her the story. The first photo showed Ashley and Lois, with Lois pointing toward the hallway leading to the offices. The second photo had Ashley holding her phone up to Lois. But the third photo, taken from a different angle, captured Lois's profile— and in her line of sight was Karl Smith, the delivery driver. I was sure they were looking right at each other.

"This photo proves he made it inside the museum," I declared. "He may have slipped and fallen, but not before making his delivery to Lois."

"To Lois?" Blanche asked.

"We met him last night," I reminded. "He told us he was looking for an L. Jones, the museum director. That had to be Lois Jones."

"That's right; the delivery was for her." She stared at the photos for a moment, focusing on them. "I'm seeing Lois later today," Blanche announced, standing up. "I'll ask her about him."

I shook my head. "She'll just tell you a story. She's not going to say what the delivery was about."

"So far, these photos don't really tell us anything other than you have a hunch—which is good—but I need more than that to run with."

"I understand, but I know there's more to this," I mumbled. I had a feeling Lois knew this man. It was the expression on her face, the glare, that was a look reserved for someone you're on a personal level with. Would Ashley know? She claimed to know her secrets.

"I hate to run, but I'm meeting with Philip Jones to interview him for the paper," Blanche said.

"Is it a good idea for you to interview him?" I asked. "You're the campaign manager for his competitor."

"Unofficial campaign manager," she smiled, flashing her pearly white teeth. "And I can be unbiased." I walked her to the front door. Butterscotch heard it open and rushed into the room. "Why don't you come with me? Take some photos?"

"I have to take Butterscotch out," I explained. "We need to go on a walk."

"That's fine. I'm meeting him in an hour at his headquarters." Blanche removed her keys from her purse. "Lois should be there...you can ask her about these photos." She winked at me before closing the door behind her. Something told me Blanche didn't believe I had anything to support my theory.

Chapter Seven

BUTTERSCOTCH and I strolled into town, a pleasant walk from our home. If I let her, Butterscotch could walk for miles and miles. I wore a pair of blue vintage capri pants, a white blouse adorned with blue polka dots, and white tennis shoes. I even found time to brush out my curls and style my hair into a cute do.

As we crossed Main Street, I spotted just the person I'd been hoping to see: Lois Jones. She stood motionless, staring into the window of a flower shop. Butterscotch caught sight of her, too, jerking her head toward Lois and coming to a halt. "Let's go see what's got her attention," I suggested, nudging her forward.

Lois didn't budge as we approached. I glanced inside the store and saw Ashley behind the counter. "Everything okay?" I asked.

Lois straightened her back and slowly turned to face me. "What?"

"Is everything alright?" I repeated. Lois was dressed in casual pants and a black sweater—an unusual look for her, as I couldn't recall ever seeing her in anything but a business suit.

Butterscotch stood beside me, her eyes fixed on Lois. I wondered about the stories she might tell me if she could talk. I smiled, recalling the look she gave me after breakfast that morning, clearly indicating I was taking too long to get ready.

Lois didn't have time for me, though. "Birdie? Don't you have somewhere else to be?"

I shrugged. "I always have time for you, Lois." I forced a smile, narrowing my lips. "We're actually on our way to the Philip Jones campaign office." I tapped my camera bag hanging from my shoulder.

Lois glared at my bag as if it were unsightly. "You are? Whatever for?"

"To take photos for the paper," I explained. "He's being interviewed."

She raised her eyebrows in surprise. "By who?"

"I thought Philip would have mentioned this to you. He has an interview with Blanche."

"No," she shook her head. "I wasn't aware of this, but Blanche has no business doing the interview." In an instant, Lois had her phone in hand. "I'll call Tennessee and have him send someone else to conduct the interview."

I shrugged again. "It's just an interview, Lois…" But the way she gripped the phone indicated she wasn't happy about this news. "Well, we better get going. I've got to get to work." Lois didn't bother to say goodbye as she hurried away. Before I could leave, Ashley tapped against the glass window of the florist shop to get my attention. She waved hello and signaled for me to wait a second.

"Birdie, Butterscotch," Ashley smiled as she joined us outside. "What a nice surprise to see you two out here! I was ordering flowers for my mother's birthday tomorrow."

"Please wish her a happy birthday from us," I replied with a smile.

"Was that Lois out here with you?" Ashley asked. "She emailed me explaining she wouldn't be at the museum today."

"She did? Why do you think she's not going to work?" I was surprised; it didn't seem to have anything to do with Philip's campaign—she hadn't even known about his interview with Moon's News.

"Lois never tells me anything unless it has to do with work at the museum," Ashley shared. Her face brightened even more as she focused on someone behind me.

"Ash," Deputy Griffins called from behind Butterscotch and me. He knelt to give Butterscotch a hearty hello, vigorously brushing her head and ears while she licked his face. "Hi, Birdie. Are you and Butters headed to Sweetie's?" He held up a paper bag marked with Sweetie's Latte logo. "I picked up your favorite, Ash—pumpkin pecan cookies, fresh out of the oven."

I quickly stepped aside as Ashley rushed in to hug him and grab the bag. "Did you happen to bring me coffee, too?" she asked, peeking inside. "I thought she was only making these during October."

"Here you go," Ben said, holding up a coffee cup with a giant smile on his friendly face. "She told me she had a special order for those cookies but had a few left over. You won't believe who I wrestled with to win those for you."

I couldn't help but laugh at the thought. "I'll let you enjoy those while they're warm." I waved goodbye as we left them in front of the floral shop, just as Ashley handed Ben a pumpkin pecan cookie.

Within minutes, we arrived at Sweetie's Latte, taking a slight detour from the campaign offices. I didn't spot Lindsay inside; she must be in the kitchen. However, I did see Stevie at the front counter, chatting with Emme, the assistant manager.

"I'm not sure how long I'll be in town," Stevie said with a

light smile. "But for sure, I'll be here over the holidays. Josh told me how magical Moon's Landing is during Christmas."

Emme nodded in agreement. "You'll have a job here as long as you want. I hope you decide to stay longer; it's been great having you."

"Thanks," Stevie smiled.

Before I could join in about how truly magical Moon's Landing is during Christmas, Doris Gilbert burst into the café, hands on her heart as she shouted, "Take that, Blanche Pruitt—I'm getting the front page of Moon's News!"

Butterscotch barked at the announcement before racing toward Doris, circling her excitedly. I hurried over to reclaim her leash, calming her down. "What happened?" I grilled. "What about the front page?"

Doris plopped down at a nearby table before answering. "I don't know what Blanche did to get herself removed from the Philip Jones interview, but Tennessee just called to inform me that I'll be handling it instead, and it'll be on the front page! Can you imagine? Doris Gilbert, Moon's News Top Reporter —with my byline! Oh, how wonderful that will look!"

I nearly fainted. How did this happen? Did I somehow cause this? "Are you sure about this?"

Doris nodded, beaming. "As sure as I am about my name. But I'll need you to go over and take some photos of him. Make sure you get him on his right side—that's his best side."

"Right side, sure." What had I done to Blanche? My heart sank.

BLANCHE DIDN'T HAVE to wait until morning to read Doris's article about Philip Jones. It went up on the Moon's News website within hours, and I was with her while she read it. We met at Sweetie's to commiserate.

"I'm so sorry. I feel like this is my fault," I declared, sharing a slice of chocolate bundt cake with her.

"It wasn't your fault," Blanche insisted, taking a bite of the cake and speaking with her mouth full. She still had that little white dog she'd named Jelly, who was tucked underneath the table, staring at Butterscotch as if trying to figure out whether she was a friend or foe. Butterscotch wagged her tail, oblivious.

"Lois was never going to let me do it," Blanche continued. "Besides, I'm supposed to be helping Lomack with his campaign—how would it have looked if I wrote that article about Jones?"

I nodded, understanding her predicament, and decided to ask about her new dog. "How are you and Jelly getting along? He seems to have taken to you quite well."

"I posted signs hoping to find his owner, but no one has

called," she replied, her brow furrowing. "I don't know what to do—I've never had a dog before. What am I supposed to do with him?" She took another bite of cake and pointed her fork at me. "I did, however, make an appointment for him at the groomers."

I sipped my latte, contemplating whether to suggest she take him to the vet for a check-up instead. "You should keep him—you've already named him, and you're the only one he likes."

"Keep him?" Her blue eyes widened in surprise. "I may not be able to afford him if I lose my job at the paper!"

"Lose your job?" I asked, taken aback. "But Tennessee can't fire you—your dad made sure that was in the contract when he sold the paper to him!"

Blanche shook her head. "Only for two years," she explained. "After that, he can fire me."

"Two years!" I couldn't believe that was part of the terms.

"Tennessee seems more than happy to replace me with Doris Gilbert. That woman tried to move into my office—thank goodness for Beaker. He's my only ally at the paper."

"But what about the rest of the staff? You hired them—I'm sure they're loyal to you."

Blanche shook her head again. "But he signs their checks, and I don't blame them. It's Christmas! No one wants to lose their job during the holidays."

As if on cue, her assistant, Beaker, burst through the café door. "Blanche!" he rushed over, slightly out of breath. "I've been looking into Philip Jones's background—like you asked." He pulled a chair from another table and sat down, which made Jelly jump out from under the table and bark, nipping at Beaker's toes.

"Wait a minute—wait a minute!" Beaker stammered, lifting his feet off the floor to avoid Jelly's sharp teeth.

"Now calm down," Blanche ordered. "Here," she held out

a treat for Jelly, who eagerly snatched it and retreated to his hiding place.

Beaker cautiously set his feet back on the floor, keeping a wary eye on Jelly. "What did you give him?"

Blanche pulled a bag of treats from her purse. "These were recommended by the clerk at the pet store. She said they have a calming effect."

"They seem to be doing their job," Beaker said with a slight chuckle.

I leaned forward and patted Beaker's hand. "Jelly just needs time to get used to us."

During the commotion, Butterscotch kept a watchful eye on Jelly. When Blanche brought out the dog treats, she couldn't resist wandering over to ask for one, and Blanche was more than happy to share.

I took a sip of my latte and then asked Beaker what he had found out about Philip Jones. He didn't disappoint.

"Jones has a very polished record," Beaker stated. "I dug and dug, but that man buried things really deep."

"But you found something?" I pressed, eager to hear the details. "What was it?"

"I thought it strange that a man with his resume was available to run in our elections—and I was right." He leaned in close, and Blanche and I mirrored his action, eager not to miss a word.

"I have a buddy from university who worked with Philip in the past. I had to call in a favor, but it was worth it," Beaker began. "Philip was being blackmailed."

"Blackmailed?" My voice rose in concern. I covered my lips with a hand and paused before asking, "What was he being blackmailed with?"

Blanche pushed the bundt cake aside. "I want to hear everything," she said, her confidence renewed.

A smile spread across Beaker's face. He leaned closer. "It

was serious—he had to resign in shame, and the allegations seemed to vanish into thin air." He flicked his fingers away as if scattering fairy dust.

"But what were the allegations?" Blanche inquired, her eyes sharp.

"Where did this happen?" I asked.

"Wait a second," Beaker held up his hands. "You won't like what I have to say. I want to be upfront about that. Blanche, to answer your question, I don't know what the allegations were—my buddy didn't know either. Only that whatever they were, they were serious enough for him to leave his post as sheriff. And Birdie, this happened three years ago in New Mexico."

"Is there anything else?" Blanche questioned, her brow furrowed.

Beaker shook his head. "No, that's all I got."

Blanche leaned back in her chair, a determined look in her eyes. "That gives me something to work with."

"Blanche? What are you going to do with this?" I asked, concern creeping into my voice.

"I'll ask him about it," she replied, her expression serious. "Give him a chance to explain his side before proceeding."

"Are you going to ask him as a reporter or as Lomack's campaign manager?" I asked.

Blanche reached for Jelly and stood up. "I need to get going. I've got a lot of work to do."

Beaker stood with her. "Anything else you need?"

Blanche shook her head. "You did great! Thank you. I'll see you tonight for dinner." Without another word, Blanche hurried out of the café, moving with a speed I'd never seen before, signaling that she was up to something.

Beaker sat back down and reached for the remaining slice of bundt cake. "You don't mind if I finish this, do you?"

I couldn't believe it—what a discovery! I pulled the photos out of my bag to look at them again. Was it possible that Karl had something to do with the blackmail? Is that why he was murdered?

AFTER LEAVING SWEETIE'S LATTE, Butterscotch and I headed to the sheriff's station. I wanted to speak to Lomack about what happened at the museum. Fortunately, he was in his office, so I let myself in.

"Birdie?" Lomack looked up from his desk. Butterscotch wasted no time; she hurried to his side and nearly jumped into his lap. "Butterscotch! How's my girl?"

I closed the door behind me, placed my camera bag on a side table, and sat across from him. His office was decked out for the holidays, with holly strung around the upper walls and golden and silver bells scattered throughout. A half-decorated Christmas tree stood in the corner, a box of ornaments lying on the floor beside it. A toy Santa perched on the edge of his desk, staring at me.

"Have you spoken to Blanche?" I wondered if she had mentioned anything about Philip Jones. Not that she would have had much time between my walk from the café to the station, but Blanche could do amazing things.

"I haven't spoken to her since last night," he said,

distracted as Butterscotch began sniffing at the Christmas tree. "Butterscotch, leave that alone."

"What about the Karl Smith case?" I inquired. "Do you have any updates?"

"What case?" Confusion crossed his face. "It has been ruled accidental."

"But it wasn't," I argued. I stood up, grabbed my camera bag, and pulled out the three photos I had shown Blanche earlier, laying them on his desk. "Take a look at these. I took them at the party. And that's not all—Karl was looking for Lois. He was delivering something to her."

"Birdie, I don't know what you're trying to get at, but these don't prove anything." Lomack picked up the photos one by one and handed them back to me. "The Karl Smith case is closed."

"But wait a minute," I said, holding the photos against my chest. "I know it doesn't look like much, but there's something here. What if I told you that he may have been blackmailing someone?" I didn't have any proof it was him—but someone was blackmailing Philip Jones.

"Blackmail? Birdie, under any other circumstances, I'd have time to listen to whatever you're angling at, but I'm on a deadline. This campaign is taking everything out of me, and I can't risk a distraction."

"But this isn't just any distraction—a man was murdered —" I stammered, defending my position.

Lomack stood up and pointed at his door. "No distractions," he stated firmly. "After this election, I'll look at this 'evidence' you have."

"But Brent—"

"That's enough. I need to get back to decorating this tree. Blanche is coming by to talk about the election, and I have a lot of work to do." He walked me to the door and held it open for me. "We can talk in a week. I'll make time for you then."

"Butterscotch," I called. She took her time walking over to me. I wouldn't let this go, but I knew a losing battle when I saw one. There was no point in trying to get through to him.

I spotted Deputy Joe Murphy at the front desk; he waved me over as he eyed Lomack's closed door. His warm brown eyes seemed heavy with concern. "He's been in there all morning. All he's asked for is coffee."

"Well, that explains a lot," I mumbled.

"What's that?" Deputy Joe questioned.

"Oh," I forced a smile. "Nothing." I followed Butterscotch over to his desk, which was neat and tidy—reminding me of Mason's desk; he, too, was very organized.

Just then, the front door of the station opened, and Josh breezed inside. The warm smile on his face was contagious, and I couldn't help but return one. He carried a bag from Sweetie's Latte. "Morning!" he proclaimed happily. "I brought bagels from Sweetie's."

Deputy Joe promptly stood up to take the bag and placed it in the coffee bar. "Thank you, Josh. I missed breakfast. This is just what we all needed."

"Hey, no problem." He paused as Butterscotch jumped up on him, resting her front paws on his shoulders as she licked his face. "There's my favorite girl."

"I didn't know the two of you were this close," I said, helping her down.

"The girl has taste," he declared, then pointed at his uncle's closed office door. "Has anyone seen him? Or has he kept himself in there since last night?"

"He's been here all night?" Now I was worried.

"This campaign's taken everything from him. My uncle won't say this, but he wants this more than anything."

"But at what cost?" I mumbled. I said goodbye to Deputy Joe and Josh before leaving the station. We crossed Main Street on our way back home.

"Birdie!" Mason called from his car parked in front of Pedro's Bistro. He waved at us before crossing the street. He patted Butterscotch on the head. "I was going to have a meeting here, but it got canceled. Would you like to join me?"

Butterscotch pulled at her leash, clearly thinking it was a good idea. "Sure." I followed her across the street, and we were immediately seated. The waiter handed me a menu, and my heart sank at the exorbitant prices. I folded the menu back up and placed it on the table. "I'd be perfectly happy grabbing something at Sweetie's."

The waiter had just begun pouring water into my goblet when he nearly spilled it at my suggestion. His lips formed two straight lines as he finished pouring Mason's glass.

"Excuse me, sir," the waiter began. "Would you like me to bring a water bowl for your hound?"

"Yes, that would be wonderful, thank you," Mason replied.

Butterscotch decided to sit beside Mason, convinced she'd have a better chance of getting table scraps from him.

"Order what you'd like," Mason suggested. "Do you have any Christmas plans? Will you be staying in town?"

Of course, where else would I be? I wondered. My parents were vacationing in Italy and wouldn't return stateside until February. They lived in their condo in Florida; if I was lucky, I saw them about twice a year. "I'm going to be here in town. Butterscotch and I are looking at trees later today. I want a big one with snow."

"You know that snow gets on everything, right?" he asked.

"But I love them," I declared. "I only wish it would snow here in Moon's Landing."

"The last time it snowed here, I believe my great-grandfather, Whiskey, was still alive," Mason said, glancing over the menu.

Daydreaming, I added, "It would be a Christmas gift if it snowed here, just once. I'd like to see it."

The waiter returned, and I ordered a salad and iced tea. Mason ordered a club sandwich with extra fries but stuck with iced water. For the rest of lunch, we discussed my Karl Smith theory.

"You believe he was murdered because he was blackmailing Jones?" He handed Butterscotch a french fry. "What did Lomack say about it?"

I put my fork down and reached for one of his fries. "He thinks it was accidental. I didn't tell him that I believe Karl was blackmailing him."

"But you believe it because of those pictures?"

I shook my head. "Not just because of the pictures. It's just a feeling I have—and I know Lois. I know something happened between her and Karl."

"Because of your hunch?" he asked. "Do you have the photos with you?"

"I do." I leaned back and reached behind me for my bag. "They're right here."

"Are these the only photos you have?" He carefully examined them.

"I have a few more in my darkroom, but these are the only ones that caught my eye as being curious," I explained.

"If you don't mind, I'd like to see the others."

His request made me think he might believe my hunch. "Of course! So you think I may be right about this?"

I felt a sense of relief at his support. After lunch, he drove us to my home, where I led him downstairs to my darkroom to retrieve the rest of the photos. I wasn't sure what we would find; I hadn't noticed anything curious about the other images, but I wouldn't mind taking another look.

I turned on the basement lights and headed toward my

worktable. "Here they are. I hope you don't mind the chemical smell. This is where I develop my photos."

"Do you prefer working with film instead of digital?" he asked, following me to the table.

"I do," I smiled. "It's simple."

"Simple?" Mason raised an eyebrow as he stood in the middle of the darkroom, surrounded by the chemicals needed to process the film, a sink that smelled of fresh water, and trays stacked against a back wall—not to mention the enlarger I used to transfer what I captured on film to paper. "I wouldn't mind learning how all of this works."

"Really?" I asked, surprised.

Mason found the additional photos I had laid out on a table. "What about these?" he asked, pointing to one. "Have you taken a look at this one?"

"Which one?" I glanced at the blurry photo he was indicating. It showed two pairs of legs. "I hadn't looked at this because it doesn't show me anything."

"Look again," he suggested. "Can you enlarge this photo?"

"Sure, but let me grab my magnifier." It wasn't anything fancy, just a regular handheld one. "These are a pair of legs standing on the top of stairs, by the look of it, a pair in shorts—wait, could this be Karl Smith? Is this a photo of Lois and Karl?"

Chapter Ten

MASON DROVE us back into town to the sheriff's station, where he dropped us off on his way back to the brewery. I wanted to show this photo to Lomack as proof I had something. But I wasn't the only one with plans to speak with him. Lois Jones was already in his office, and the door was firmly closed. I didn't want to wait for a private moment; I couldn't. I pushed open the door, interrupting them.

"I have to show you this photo, Deputy Lomack," I proclaimed, holding it up.

Lois was seated across from Lomack, she was dressed in a sharp red business suit. "I hope you take this situation seriously," she said, her eyes narrowing at me—she clearly didn't appreciate my interruption. "What is this about? Can't you see we are having a private conversation?"

"Yes," I replied, my resolve firm. "But this is important. It's about the Karl Smith murder case."

"Birdie." The way Lomack said my name should have warned me not to press this further, but I couldn't just drop it.

Ignoring him, I held the photo up near my face. "This photo proves Lois had something to do with Karl's accident. It shows them speaking to each other."

"What do you have there?" Lois stood and snatched the photo from my hand, glaring at it. "What is this about? I thought this had been ruled accidental."

"It has," Lomack assured her. "Birdie, I told you the case was closed. Leave that here, and please leave my office."

Lois gripped the photo so tightly that the paper curled. "If you print this in the paper you work for, I will sue you and it into oblivion." With that threat, she crumpled the photo in her fist and tossed it on the floor. Turning back to Lomack, she pointed a polished finger at him. "And you—I will make you look the fool...not that you don't already." She pushed past me as she stormed out of his office.

"Birdie, what were you thinking, accusing her like that?" Lomack demanded.

I didn't have an answer—at least not one he would appreciate. Butterscotch gave me a pitiful look, as though she understood I was in trouble with Lomack, a man she considered family because he had once dated my aunt Lula. "I'm sorry. I didn't mean for it to get out of hand."

Lomack reached for the crumpled photograph and handed it back to me. "I know how you feel about Lois, but you're out of line here."

I shook my head, unwilling to argue. He had made up his mind about this case, but that didn't mean it was over. "I'm sorry about this," I said. "Come on, Butterscotch, let's go." Lomack held the door open for me, clearly hoping I would let this case drop.

"It's Christmas, Birdie. Enjoy the season. Don't let this case consume everything for you. Trust me, there have been cases that took over my life. Do you know what happened? I missed out on living."

I nodded, understanding, but this wasn't like his other cases—far from it! I decided I needed to talk to Mason. I was sure he had connections that could help. I needed to speak with him.

Chapter Eleven

But Mason had left Moon's Landing on business, and his assistant didn't know when he'd return. My call to his cell phone went straight to voicemail. With no other leads, I headed to Moon's News to track down Blanche, who was also avoiding my calls.

I found her in a conference room with her assistant, Beaker. They were pinning photos on a board. From where I stood in the doorway, I couldn't see who—or what—was in the pictures.

Butterscotch barked, jolting them both out of concentration. They turned, startled.

"Oh, Birdie, it's just you," Blanche gasped, hand over her heart.

I stepped in and shut the door behind me. "What are you two working on in here?"

Beaker pointed at the board. "Trying to piece together what happened at the museum."

Blanche sat down, rifling through papers on the table. "For a second, I thought you were Doris. She's been sneaking around that door all afternoon, trying to grab a look inside."

"She has?" I chuckled, glancing at Beaker for confirmation.

He nodded. "You just missed her by fifteen minutes."

"Missed her? But the door was open when I came in." I raised an eyebrow. "Did one of you leave it open?"

Blanche shot Beaker a sharp look. "I thought you were keeping an eye on the door?"

He shook his head. "I thought you were."

"I've been going over our notes." She huffed, then turned to me. "Why don't you pull up a chair? We've got plenty to catch you up on."

Butterscotch, sensing no immediate danger, trotted over to sniff Blanche's and Beaker's hands in search of treats. Beaker, ever prepared, offered her a cookie from his bag before suggesting, "Why don't I get her a few more from my office stash?"

"Where's Jelly?" I asked Blanche, looking around for her new dog.

"At daycare," she replied with a sigh. "Better for him while I'm in and out of meetings all day."

"You took Jelly to daycare?" I laughed, and she shrugged.

"Desperate times." She waved me over to her stack of papers. "We were going over what we discussed. Lois is definitely connected to what happened with Karl Smith."

"You believe me?" My pulse quickened as I scanned the papers. "What did you find?"

Blanche tapped a folder. "It's not just about Lois. Beaker got some dirt on Philip, too. It seems this person was blackmailing him." She handed me a letter bearing Philip's name. "This is from someone named Jade Clementine, demanding fifteen thousand dollars or they'd 'go to the press with everything.'"

I scanned the document, eyebrows raised. "Fifteen thousand dollars? What could Jade have had on him?"

"That was just the beginning. Apparently, Jade upped it to twenty thousand in the next letter." Blanche took a few letters from my hands and spread them on the table.

"How did Beaker's friend get ahold of these?" I asked, amazed. "And do you think Jade could be an alias Karl Smith used?" I still believed that Karl was the one who had been blackmailing Philip.

"They were sent anonymously to several city council members, prompting an emergency meeting." Blanche gathered the papers back into the folder. "I suppose it very well could have been Karl who sent them."

"What happened at the city council meeting?"

"Philip resigned. I have an unofficial meeting tomorrow with Douglas Clark, one of the council members who attended."

I smirked, sensing Blanche's signature strategy. "Unofficial? Does Douglas know he has a meeting with you?"

"Not yet, but I know where he grabs coffee every morning."

"Well, this is enough to shut down Philip's campaign. He might even leave town for good." I crossed my arms, thinking about how this could help Lomack's chances. "We'll have a new sheriff by Christmas."

Blanche's expression remained cautious. "I wouldn't be so sure. Lois could still spin this and make Philip look like the victim."

Her phone buzzed, and she glanced at it.

"Expecting a call?" I asked, noticing her expression.

She tucked her phone away. "I haven't told Tennessee about this yet. He wants to be informed of everything I work on, but if I tell him, he'll shut it down."

Her words reminded me of my own encounter with Lois at Lomack's office. I wanted to tell her about it, but before I could speak, the door swung open, and Lindsay walked in, holding a box from her café.

"Thought you might be hungry," she said cheerfully. "Beaker mentioned you were settling in for a long night, so I doubled your order."

"Lindsay, you're a lifesaver!" Blanche lit up, peeking inside. "You even brought cookies."

"I know about your sweet tooth," Lindsay chuckled. Then she turned to me, raising an eyebrow. "Birdie, you look pleased with yourself. Did you and Blanche uncover something?"

"Maybe." Blanche looked away sheepishly. "But you know we can't say." Her phone buzzed again. "It's doggy daycare. I have to go pick up Jelly."

"You're not bringing him back here, are you?" Lindsay asked with a touch of concern. "This is no place for him. You should take him home and get settled in. Have you bought him a bed yet?"

"A bed?" Blanche raised eyebrows in confusion.

I intervened, sensing a practical solution. "Why don't we all head to your place, Blanche? We can go over this without worrying about Doris sneaking in."

Blanche's eyes widened. "Are you saying you'll help?"

"Isn't that what I've been doing?" I winked at Lindsay and gestured to the food. "How much did you pack in there?"

Chapter Twelve

Before I knew it, Blanche, Butterscotch, and I were parked in front of Philip Jones's campaign office. I shot Blanche a sideways look as I waited for an explanation.

"What are we doing here? I thought we were going to pick up Jelly before heading to your place."

She shrugged, unbuckling her seatbelt. "What's wrong with one little stop?" She flashed a sly smile. "It won't take long."

The lights were off inside the office, giving the impression it was empty. "It doesn't look like anyone's here, Blanche. Why don't we just go pick up Jelly?"

Butterscotch, squeezed onto my lap in Blanche's compact car, pawed eagerly at the door. Blanche hopped out and left the door open just long enough for Butterscotch to follow.

"Wait!" I called, but Blanche only smiled as she zipped up her jacket. I had a feeling she was up to no good. "We are not going inside." I climbed out, closing the car door a little too forcefully. If Blanche wanted to get into a place, she'd find a way. "Come on, let's grab coffee instead and talk this out."

"It won't take long, I promise." She waved off my

concerns. "You and Butterscotch, keep an eye out and text me if you see anything suspicious."

"And the alarm? Or the cameras?" I whispered urgently, glancing up at the building. "Someone's bound to see us parked right out front!"

Blanche gave a dismissive wave. "I know what I'm doing."

I sighed, realizing there was no talking her out of it. Leave it to Blanche to want every last piece of evidence against Philip Jones, even if we already had enough to end his campaign. I tried one last protest, but she only turned to shush me, saying I was "making too much noise."

"Come on, Butterscotch," I whispered to my coonhound. "Let's hide behind that tree."

Butterscotch had other plans. Ignoring my command, she trotted happily after Blanche, slipping right through the door as Blanche jimmied the lock open. The lights flicked on, and I knew we were in trouble.

"Blanche!" I hissed. "We have to go."

I dashed inside, trying to grab Butterscotch's collar. Unfortunately, I hadn't thought to bring her leash when we piled out of Blanche's car.

Butterscotch, however, thought we were playing a game. She darted in circles around the office, her tail wagging furiously. She crouched, leaning on her back legs, and then skidded across the floor, running laps around the desks.

"Butterscotch! Come here," I called, trying to corner her, but she was too quick.

"I'll get her," Blanche offered, not sounding overly concerned. She veered off to a desk, pulled open a drawer, and began rummaging through it.

"What are you doing?" I demanded, grabbing for Butterscotch as she zipped past. "We need to leave—now!"

"Alright, alright." Frustrated, Blanche slammed the drawer shut. "Butterscotch, I've got cookies in the car—let's go!"

The promise of treats finally stopped Butterscotch, who bolted to the front door just as red and blue lights flashed down the street. Two patrol cars were approaching.

"Looks like we did trigger an alarm." I crossed my arms, giving Blanche a glare. "How exactly are you going to talk us out of getting arrested?"

Butterscotch sat beside me, panting happily, looking rather pleased with herself. I shot Blanche a pointed look. "You just got my dog arrested."

"Don't worry," she said confidently. "I'm not letting my best friend and her dog get hauled off to jail. I'm sure that's Deputy Joe and Griffins—no way they're going to arrest us. They'll probably just send us off to Sweetie's."

A patrol car rolled to a stop in front of us. Blanche was right—up to a point. But as the officer stepped out, I felt my confidence slip. Deputy Lomack slammed his car door, his face illuminated by the police lights, and he didn't look pleased.

Blanche raised her hands in a quick surrender, and I did the same, leaning close. "I think we're about to be arrested," I whispered.

Butterscotch, oblivious, ran up to Lomack, planting her big paws on his shoulders and giving him a sloppy kiss. She then hopped into his patrol car, putting her paw on the steering wheel as if about to honk the horn.

The second patrol car parked behind Lomack's. At least Blanche had been half-right—Deputy Griffins stepped out, smiling and giving us a little wave. "Another murder?" he asked with a chuckle before containing himself to ask, "What's going on with all the serious faces?"

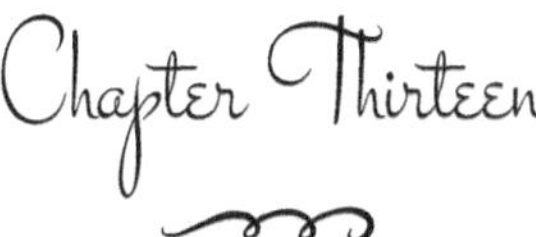

Chapter Thirteen

MY PHONE CALL had been to Mason, but it went straight to voicemail. A pit of dread settled in my stomach as I pictured the three of us spending the night in jail. Butterscotch jumped up beside me, sensing my distress. I patted her head, wrapping my arms around her and burying my face in her fur.

"It's going to be fine," Blanche reassured me. "I still have my phone call, and I promise I'll get us out of here before you know it."

"Blanche, I don't think you understand. We broke into a campaign office—and you're the campaign manager for the rival!"

"Unofficial campaign manager," she corrected, shrugging. "And I'll tell Lomack you had nothing to do with it. You didn't even know where we were going until it was too late."

Just then, Deputy Joe walked in and stood in front of our cell, his usually warm brown eyes now serious and downcast. "I'm sorry to see you ladies in here," he said, voice somber, "especially so close to Christmas."

Blanche flashed him a charming smile. "Deputy Joe, this

was all a misunderstanding! Let me out, and I'll explain everything to Lomack."

Butterscotch and I stayed seated on the cot as Deputy Joe shook his head. "I'm afraid I can't do that. I'm here on official business."

"Is it time for my phone call?" Blanche asked, looking at me with a confident nod. "I'll call Beaker and have him pay our bail."

But Deputy Joe unlocked the cell door and called Butterscotch over. I stood up, alarmed. "Where are you taking her?"

"No need to worry." He closed the door behind her, the lock clicking sharply, as if emphasizing our situation. "She's just going to be in Deputy Lomack's care until you're released."

"What?" I gripped the bars. "For how long?"

"Only until you're out. It's for the best, Birdie." His face looked crestfallen.

Butterscotch barked at me as she trotted to the door, seemingly unbothered—though I couldn't blame her. "Can you make sure she gets dinner?"

Deputy Joe nodded, a small smile breaking his serious expression. "I'll see to it." He followed Butterscotch out, leaving Blanche and me alone in the cell. I sank back onto the cot.

Blanche sat beside me. "It's going to be fine," she insisted. "Beaker will use the emergency fund I've got set aside—he'll have us out in an hour, maybe two."

I shot her a look. "How many times have you been arrested that you actually have a fund for it?"

She bit her lip, getting up to press against the cell door as though trying to peer out the window—not that she could see anything from there. "Maybe once, maybe four times," she mumbled.

Deputy Griffins opened the door, smiling. "Blanche, it's your turn to make your call."

"Yes!" she said, shooting me a wink before following Griffins out.

The cell felt empty after they left, though I hoped Blanche would work her magic. I took a deep breath and leaned against the cold brick wall, closing my eyes and waiting.

The silence in the cell seemed to magnify every sound—the tick of the clock above the door, the click of a ceiling fan that spun outside my cell, threatening to fly off at any moment.

Finally, I stood and went to the bars, gripping them as I tried to see out the small window in the main door. What's taking so long? Just as I was about to give up, the door opened, and Blanche returned with Deputy Griffins.

"Looks like you're in luck, Birdie," Deputy Griffins said with a grin. "You're free to go."

"So fast?" I asked, glancing at Blanche in surprise, though I was happy enough to leave without an explanation. I just needed to find Butterscotch, and I'd be on my way.

Then Tennessee Langford stepped through the door, wearing a smug smile. "Hello, Birdie. Just wanted to make sure you knew I'm the one who got the two of you out of here."

"You?" I asked, bewildered.

Griffins unlocked the cell door, gesturing for me to step out. "Don't keep the man waiting. He managed to get the Joneses to drop the charges."

"He did?" I glanced between Blanche and Tennessee, waiting for someone to explain.

Blanche's expression was unreadable—a clear sign she wasn't happy. What had gone on between her and Tennessee?

Griffins filled in the silence. "Lois and Philip just left, but I heard something about an apology on the front page of *Moon's News.*"

"What?" I turned to Blanche, hoping for confirmation.

Tennessee cleared his throat. "We'll discuss it in the morning, first thing at the office."

I didn't like the sound of that—it felt a little too official. Was I about to lose my job—again?

Chapter Fourteen

It's Christmas Eve and election Day, just days after my meeting with Tennessee. I was still on as the paper's photographer, but officially "on notice." Tennessee made it clear that he didn't want any more late-night calls from the police station about his employees getting arrested for breaking and entering.

I was relieved he hadn't fired me, but I couldn't shake my curiosity. What had gone down between Tennessee, Lois, and Philip? It had to be more than just printing an apology. He hadn't shared the details with me, but ever since we got out, Blanche had been unusually quiet.

Mason was still out of town on business. He texted me earlier, simply: "Back in town today. M."

I took Butterscotch on a walk toward City Hall to vote, although I felt a pang of guilt thinking about the election. Had we doomed Brent Lomack's campaign with our "shenanigans"? A line of voters stretched outside the building, and I watched as an older woman exited, proudly affixing an "I Voted" sticker on her lapel.

Lindsay Zimmer stepped up behind the woman. They

exchanged good mornings, and the woman told Lindsay she'd see her at Sweetie's.

"Lindsay!" I waved to catch her attention. She spotted us and came down the steps, her smile as bright as her pink shirt with a fresh sticker already on it.

"Good morning, you two!" she chirped, reaching out to pet Butterscotch, who was already pawing at her for attention. "I hope I see you at Sweetie's this morning—I've got a fresh batch of doggy cookies waiting for her."

"Butterscotch wouldn't miss it," I assured her, smiling. "She never passes up treats."

Lindsay leaned in, lowering her voice. "I also have a few peppermint cherry tarts waiting for you." She gave Butterscotch one more pat before leaving.

But the line didn't budge. People trickled out from voting, so why weren't we moving? Butterscotch looked up at me, as if expecting me to do something about it.

"Birdie!" Blanche's voice called from the sidewalk as she jogged over. "It took forever to find a parking spot."

A man in line grumbled about "line cutters" but didn't say more. Blanche ignored him, greeting Butterscotch before falling into step with us. Twenty minutes passed before we neared the voting booth. Philip Jones was just leaving, giving me an odd look as he passed. Lois, right behind him, walked over just as the attendant handed me my ballot.

"I want to personally thank you," she said, a tight smile on her lips. "Without your little break-in, we wouldn't be leading in the polls."

Blanche, standing midway to the voting booth, quickly returned and took my arm, steering me forward. "Let's go vote, Birdie. Good morning, Lois. I'm sure we'll see you at Sweetie's later."

Lois folded her arms, giving a sharp little laugh. "You'll never catch me there. The food is much too dry for my taste."

Butterscotch gave a low, deep growl. I quickly tugged her along. "Let's go vote, Butterscotch."

Blanche sighed as we reached the booth. "Lois is still bitter about her uncle dropping the charges," she whispered. "Tennessee told me it was a nightmare convincing her, but her uncle agreed as long as Tennessee killed my story."

"I'm sorry about that," I said softly. "But what else did the two of you talk about? Did you tell him about the blackmail? About Karl—"

"He wouldn't listen even if I brought up all of that. But it doesn't mean I'm done with it," she grinned. "I've got an article ready to go once this election is over."

"You do?" I asked, though it didn't surprise me.

"Excuse me, ladies," an attendant called out, frowning. "No talking in the polling area."

I gave Blanche a sheepish look and cast my ballot. The names of Philip Jones and Brent Lomack were printed clearly. The choice was simple, and I checked Lomack's name before handing my ballot back to the attendant, who thanked me and gave me a sticker.

"Do you have lollipops instead?" Blanche asked over my shoulder.

The attendant gave her a stern look as she handed Blanche her sticker. Once outside, Blanche told me she'd meet us at Sweetie's but had to make a quick stop first.

"Where are you headed?" I asked, curious about what could be more important than Sweetie's.

She lowered her voice, glancing around. "I'll tell you later," she said with a sly grin, then hurried off.

"She's up to something," I whispered to Butterscotch as we followed her.

Blanche hadn't taken her car and was heading down the street away from City Hall. She stopped in front of Mason's microbrewery, glancing around before stepping inside. Butterscotch tugged on her leash, eager to follow, but I held her close, wondering what to do.

My curiosity won out. Before I knew it, Butterscotch and I were at the door, but the *Closed* sign hung prominently on it. I gave Butterscotch's leash a gentle tug. "Looks like we won't be following her after all."

Chapter Fifteen

BLANCHE DIDN'T RESURFACE for the rest of the day. That evening, Butterscotch and I settled into the living room, me with a cup of coffee topped with peppermint whipped cream, and her in her bed by the sofa, paws clutching her favorite chew toy. I flipped on the TV, nerves twisting in my stomach while waiting for the election results.

The reporter on screen was talking with Philip Jones, asking about his expectations. He smiled into the camera but didn't answer, simply thanking the reporter for braving the cold to support him. Then, the scene shifted back to the news-room, where a pair of news anchors were seated.

"We have the results!" Debra Smiley announced, glancing at the co-anchor beside her. "So, Jared, who do you think the winner is?"

Jared Forswright grinned, arching a dramatic eyebrow. "No favorites here, but I do have the results." He held up a sealed envelope. "Just handed over by our producer." He opened it, read it, and passed the results to Debra.

She glanced at the card, then looked into the camera,

beaming. "You won't believe this—Deputy Brent Lomack is now the Sheriff of Moon's Landing!"

"Debra," Jared teased, "something tells me you voted for him."

She held up the card for the camera to reveal Lomack's name. "It's official!"

I reached for my phone to call Blanche, but it started ringing just as I grabbed it.

"Birdie!" Blanche's voice burst over the line on the second ring. "Bring your camera and meet me at the sheriff's station!"

She hung up before I could respond. I hugged Butterscotch, kissing her on the brow. "Brent won!" I whispered, before gathering my gear and ordering a cab, leaving Butterscotch at home to enjoy her toy.

The ride felt shorter than usual, maybe because of my excitement. When I arrived, Boston Bob was stepping out of the station, holding the door open for me. I jumped a little, caught off guard.

"Oh," I said, smiling. "I didn't expect to see you here."

"Evening, Birdie." He tilted his baseball cap, moving to leave.

On impulse, I caught his arm, curiosity getting the better of me. "Did you have anything to do with Lomack winning?"

Boston Bob paused, then leaned closer. "That would be Sheriff Lomack," he corrected, a twinkle in his eye. "And let's just say it might be the first time in a long time the Society of Sanitation has made an appearance at the polls."

A slow smile spread across my face. "And why would the S.O.S. suddenly be voting?"

Bob shrugged, giving me a conspiratorial wink. "Simple. Moon's Landing isn't keen on strangers coming in and changing things. We like things as they are, and I wasn't about to let some outsider come in and ruffle our feathers—would you?"

"But what about—"

"Now, don't ask too many questions, Birdie," he grinned. "Just enjoy the win. I know I will." With that, he gave a playful nod and sauntered off, a kick in his step.

Blanche rushed out of the station, her eyes shining. "Birdie, we have so much to do. Come on!"

Inside, balloons filled every corner, and a giant balloon arch stretched over the main desk. Lomack was ordering Deputy Joe to take them down, muttering, "This is a sheriff's station, not a gift shop." He turned to Blanche, sighing. "Will you help him clear this up?"

"Congratulations, Sheriff Lomack!" I called, loud enough to be heard over the popping of balloons. I thought briefly of asking him about the Karl Smith case but decided to hold off.

Lomack gave me a nod before gesturing for Blanche to join him in his office, closing the door behind them.

Deputy Griffins sighed as he popped a balloon. "He's not one for celebrations."

"Want help with those?" I asked.

He shook his head. "Actually, why don't I give you a ride home?" He smiled knowingly. "I can tell you, Lomack would rather spend the night with his feet up than deal with all this fuss."

I glanced toward the closed office door. "Blanche did ask me to take a photo of him for the paper."

Griffins chuckled. "Trust me, he'll be just fine without it."

I texted Blanche that I was heading out, then accepted his offer for a ride home. As soon as we were in the patrol car, I couldn't resist bringing up the Karl Smith case.

"What do you think happened that night?"

Griffins gave me a sideways smile as he pulled onto the road. "I heard your theory. Can't say I disagree."

"You *agree*?" I gasped, surprised. "Lomack told me he thought I didn't have anything."

He shrugged, his expression thoughtful. "But the question is, how do you prove it?"

I hesitated, then asked, "Have you talked to Ashley? She works with Lois, so maybe she's heard something."

Griffins chuckled. "Ashley mentioned she knows some of Lois's secrets, but that's putting it lightly. And, no, she hasn't told me anything specific. But if she did…" He trailed off, glancing at me pointedly.

I leaned back, nodding. "Fair enough."

After a pause, I added, "Do you know where Ashley is now?"

He nodded. "She's at the museum."

I straightened up. "Can you drive me there instead of home? I'd love to talk to her."

With a grin, he reached for the patrol car's switch. "How about I run the lights?"

I laughed as he flipped on the flashing reds and blues. "I won't tell Lomack about this," I promised, settling in for the ride to the museum.

Chapter Sixteen

GRIFFINS WAITED by his patrol car as I made my way into the museum. He'd already called Ashley to let her know we were coming and that I had a few questions for her. She sounded amused but said she'd leave the side door open. Sure enough, she was waiting for me.

"Hi, Birdie," she called from a conference room. "I'm in here."

"Thanks for meeting with me," I said, stepping into the doorway. "I think you might be able to help me with the Karl Smith case."

"I didn't know there was one." Ashley was bent over a table, eyeing several swatches of wallpaper. "I'm planning for a new exhibit. But I can spare a few minutes." She gestured to a chair for me to sit on, but she remained standing.

"I won't take up much of your time," I assured her, moving into the room and setting my camera bag on the chair. "Did Karl Smith make regular deliveries here—for Lois?"

She shook her head. "I never saw him before that night, but I'm not surprised if he was here for Lois."

"You're not?" I asked, taken aback. "I think she may have been involved in his death."

Ashley straightened, her fingers tapping the back of her chair, one hand on her hip. She looked remarkably unfazed, as if these conversations were routine for her. "Lois isn't the kind of person you'd want to question about these things, Birdie. You might not like where it leads."

"But I need to know what happened. Lois can't just walk away from this—"

"It wouldn't be the first time," Ashley said, almost casually. Her gaze was steady, detached, and I wondered how much more she knew than she was letting on.

I decided it was best to be direct. "I overheard you tell Lois you knew her secrets. You didn't seem scared of her."

Ashley paused, then reached into a bag, pulling out a sealed envelope with my name on it. "She told me you'd be by and asked me to give this to you."

"What's this?" I took the envelope from her, resisting the urge to tear it open on the spot.

Ashley offered me a sympathetic smile. "I wish I could chat more, but I'm on a tight deadline."

"Wait," I said, feeling the urgency rise. "I understand if you don't want to talk about that night, but Karl Smith's family deserves answers."

"And I would agree," she replied, "but the only people who'll ever know the full truth are Lois and Karl—and guess which one can talk about it?"

"That's... a little cold," I replied, immediately regretting the bluntness. Ashley's expression hardened.

I took a breath, trying a different angle. "I have photos of Lois with him that night. And I know Philip Jones was black-mailed out of his old job—"

"Why don't you read her note?" Ashley suggested,

gesturing to the envelope. "With Lois gone, I have plenty to handle."

"Gone? You mean… resigned?" I asked, glancing down at the envelope before opening it. Inside was a card with a short, chilling message.

Birdie,

Please take this as my goodbye to you and Moon's Landing. Don't try looking for me. You won't be able to find me. But know this: you will lose everything when you least expect it.

I don't make empty promises.

Lois

I looked up, startled. "Lois has really left?"

"She cleared out her desk twenty minutes before you got here." Ashley walked me back to the door, her expression serious. "Trust me on this, Birdie: let it go. I know what Lois is capable of, and if you keep pushing, she'll make sure you regret it."

"Why are you protecting her?" I asked, suddenly frustrated. "You know more than you're saying—don't you?"

Ashley hesitated. "Yes," she admitted quietly, clearing her throat. "But I'm not ready to share it. Not yet."

I left Ashley in the conference room and walked down the hall to Lois's old office. I needed to see for myself that she was really gone. The door stood open, but the office wasn't empty —Philip Jones was there, seated behind her desk, flipping a pen between his fingers. He didn't look up as I paused in the doorway, but he knew I was there.

"I gave up everything for her," he muttered.

"What was that?" I asked, stepping further into the room. "Where did Lois go?"

He shrugged, looking up to meet my eyes. "I don't know, and I don't care."

"I don't believe that," I replied, watching him closely. "Why would Lois leave? Unless she's running from something."

He stopped flipping the pen and slapped it down on the desk. "She's running because of me."

"From you?" I asked, startled. "Why would she be running from you? What happened with Karl Smith?"

"I didn't do anything," he said quickly. "But Lois wouldn't let him go. Not after he started threatening her."

"Threatening her?" This was a surprise—I'd assumed Philip was the one being blackmailed. "Who was Karl blackmailing? And who is Jade—"

"Karl!" Philip interrupted, his voice sharp. "Karl is Jade. But none of that matters now. Don't you see? This was all about you."

"Me?" I felt a chill as he nodded, his face unreadable.

"Lois did all of this to get back at you—and your aunt Lula," he said, the bitterness in his voice unmistakable. "She told me that if I came here and became sheriff, we could help each other. I needed a new start, and she wanted you out of her way."

My head spun with this revelation. "So, all of this...because of me?"

Philip nodded, clearly struggling with the weight of his confession. "Karl—Jade—whoever he was, was blackmailing me. He knew I'd done some... underhanded things in New Mexico when I was sheriff. Things I won't get into. Lois thought she could make him disappear, but we didn't know who he really was—not until he showed up here, at the party."

I felt my stomach drop. "How did he know to find you here?"

"Lois orchestrated everything," he said grimly. "She didn't tell me exactly how, but she promised he'd reveal himself. Only, he wasn't supposed to show up that night. He came early—probably couldn't resist the chance to squeeze us for more."

"Then why did she leave now?"

Philip stood, pushing his chair back and straightening. "Because I told her that losing the election was a wake-up call, and I was going to Lomack to tell him everything."

I blinked, surprised. "You're going to Lomack?"

He nodded firmly. "It's beyond time," he said, the resolve clear in his voice. "So, she ran... but where she went? I have no idea."

Chapter Seventeen

It was Christmas morning, and the doorbell woke me from a restless sleep. Butterscotch started barking at the first ring, and I slipped on my robe and slippers, feeling the weight of a long, sleepless night spent on the phone with Blanche. We'd talked for hours about Lois—wondering what had happened to her, where she might be hiding, and if she'd ever return to Moon's Landing.

I opened the door, surprised to find Mason standing on my porch. "Mason?" I murmured, rubbing the sleep from my eyes. "What time is it?"

He smiled and handed me a cup of coffee from Sweetie's Latte before gently pulling me outside. The chill in the air hit me, but something else did too—I hadn't noticed it at first, but tiny, glistening flakes began to drift around us. One landed on my nose, and I tilted my head to look up at the morning sky.

"Snow?" I breathed, staring at the flakes in wonder. But something about it wasn't quite right. They were softer, lighter, and shimmered like little bubbles in the faint light.

Mason grinned, pulling me further into the yard as he

spun me around, dancing to a Christmas song that floated from his open garage. Butterscotch barked and leapt around the yard, snapping playfully at the "snow" with her tail wagging wildly.

I held out my hand to catch a flake, watching it dissolve. These weren't snowflakes at all! They were translucent, airy bubbles, gently drifting down. The song ended, and a voice crackled over the radio, "Merry Christmas, Moon's Landing! And yes, it does appear to be snowing—but it's not real snow. We had a little mishap at the microbrewery this morning, and bubbles are shooting up into the sky! Let's enjoy this 'snow' and pretend along with me, won't you? I'm sure Mason Moon will explain it all tomorrow morning."

I looked up at him, heartwarming in the early morning light. "You made it snow?"

He dropped his gaze, a soft smile playing at his lips. "I had some help from Blanche. She told me you were following her that morning after the election. We agreed you needed a little Christmas magic."

So *that* was why Blanche was sneaking around the microbrewery that day. I couldn't help but laugh.

Mason leaned close, his breath warm against my ear. "Merry Christmas..." he whispered, pulling me closer as the bubbles drifted around us, turning the yard into a sparkling, enchanted wonderland.

About the Author

Shelley Weiss is a dreamer of all things magical. She loves to write poems and drink coffee. When she's not writing, she's working on her endless sewing projects and reading books. She and her husband live in Southern California with their menagerie of pets.

If you wish to be notified about her next book or giveaway, sign up for her mailing list at

Shelley's Newsletter!
or visit
www.shelleyweiss.com